S0-BOT-043

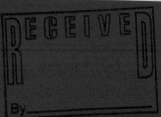

MARVEL

MILES MORALES SPIDER-MAN

THROUGH A HERO'S EYES

Written by
DENENE MILLNER

Pictures by
MÓNICA PAOLA RODRÍGUEZ

MARVEL

Los Angeles • New York

FOR CHILDREN WHO TELL THE STORIES AND SING THE
SONGS OF THEIR ANCESTORS' TONGUE, KNOWING THAT
THIS LAND AND THAT LAND, TOO, ARE BOTH HOME
—DENENE

TO ALL THE BORINQUEÑOS, PA' QUE TU LO SEPAS!
—MONICA

MARVEL

First Edition, November 2023

10 9 8 7 6 5 4 3 2 1

FAC-034274-23257

Printed in the United States of America

This book is set in Charter Roman and Flicker Regular

Designed by Emily Fisher

Library of Congress Control Number: 2020937176

ISBN 978-1-368-06072-1

Reinforced binding

Visit www.DisneyBooks.com and www.Marvel.com

This is **MILES MORALES**. He lives in a Brooklyn neighborhood full of one of his favorite things: art. Miles loves to draw in his free time, but he doesn't have much of that these days. That's because Miles has a secret.

Miles is SPIDER-MAN.

Nearly every evening, when the sun sinks down and the city's lights start twinkling, Miles swings across the skyline.

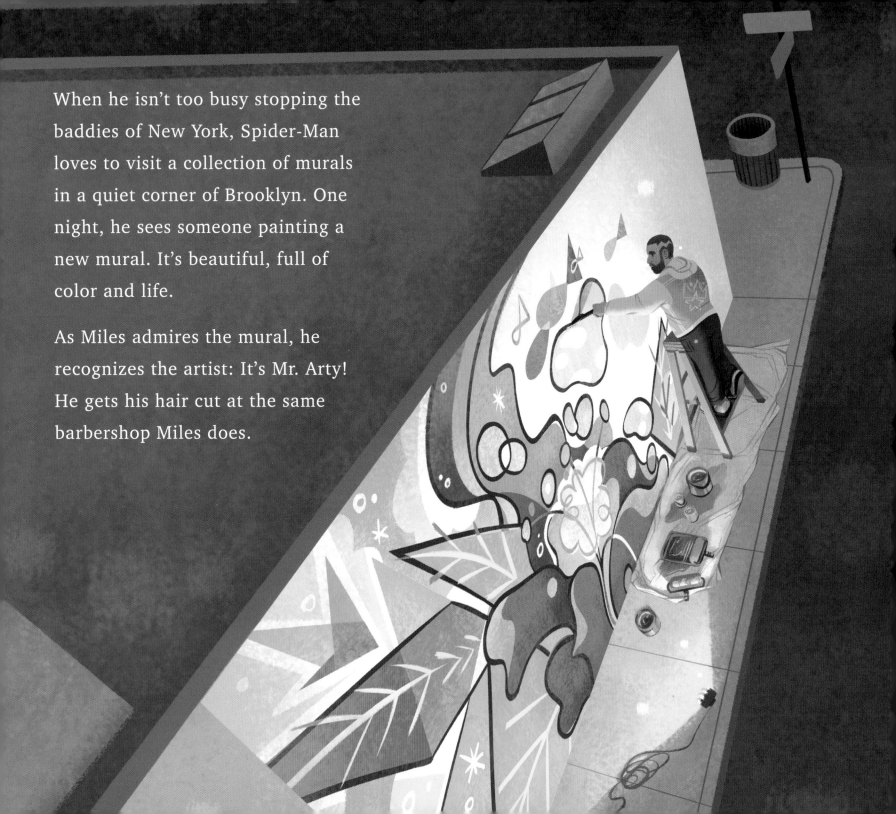

When he isn't too busy stopping the baddies of New York, Spider-Man loves to visit a collection of murals in a quiet corner of Brooklyn. One night, he sees someone painting a new mural. It's beautiful, full of color and life.

As Miles admires the mural, he recognizes the artist: It's Mr. Arty! He gets his hair cut at the same barbershop Miles does.

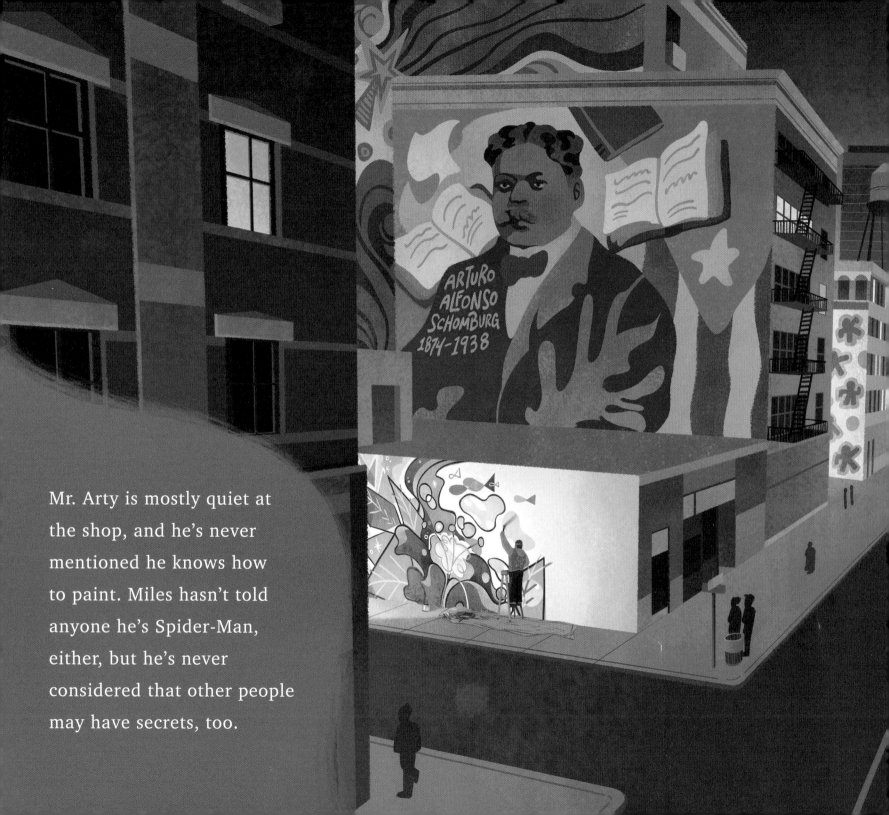

Mr. Arty is mostly quiet at the shop, and he's never mentioned he knows how to paint. Miles hasn't told anyone he's Spider-Man, either, but he's never considered that other people may have secrets, too.

The next Thursday afternoon, Miles walks through the Cutz's Swag Shop door to a welcoming chorus. His barber, Cutz, snaps a fresh towel across his chair. Getting a cut from **THE** Cutz makes Miles feel like he's sitting on a throne.

"Hey, Miles!" Cutz yells.

Miles catches Mr. Arty's eye in the mirror and nods hello, but Mr. Arty ignores him. Mr. Arty hardly ever talks in the barbershop.

Miles listens to the familiar sounds of loud opinions and even louder laughter drifting through the shop. Cutz's Swag Shop is where he gets his best lessons on how to BE.

Cutz points to a poster and tells Miles, "I took the kids to the museum to see the new Basquiat exhibit."

"Those crowns in his paintings are tight, but I don't know about those skeleton heads he painted all over his art," says Black.

"All you need to know is that Basquiat is **THE** man," says Cutz.

"Basquiat is okay, but he's no Romare Bearden!" says Mojo.

Suddenly, Mr. Arty speaks.

"Art is more than pretty pictures. It's a celebration of culture and life and the artists who make it. Barely anyone knows that Basquiat has puertorriqueño running in his veins."

"My mami taught me that same thing. Basquiat is one of my favorite artists," Miles says proudly.

Before long, the whole shop is buzzing with small facts and big truths about Puerto Rican culture.

"Puerto Rico has some of the most beautiful beaches you ever seen!" someone exclaims.

"Outside of Puerto Rico, you won't find better mofongo than right here in Brooklyn. You better ask somebody," another says boldly.

"Look around you. Puerto Rico is everywhere," someone adds.

Miles's mom is puertorriqueña, and she's taught him all about her culture—his culture. But he's never heard anyone talk about Puerto Rico and art the way Mr. Arty does.

When Cutz finishes the last swipe of Miles's hair, Miles hands the barber a ten-dollar bill and follows Mr. Arty out of the shop. "Hey, Mr. Arty!" yells Miles.

"You know a lot about art. Are you an artist?" Miles asks. Mr. Arty grunts and walks faster, so Miles speeds up, too. "I'm half–Puerto Rican, like Basquiat, and I like to draw. I want to be an artist someday."

Mr. Arty sizes up Miles, like he's seeing him for the first time. "Well, loving art is a good thing," Mr. Arty says, slowing his pace. "What do you like about it?"

They talk about art as they walk, and Mr. Arty offers Miles some advice. "You should always be paying attention. A true artist knows that everywhere you go, there's always something to learn." But Miles isn't listening anymore. His spider-sense is going WILD.

"LOOK OUT!" Miles shouts. Three thieves, known as the Enforcers, run past Miles and Mr. Arty. Miles makes sure Mr. Arty is okay while quickly saying, "I'm sorry, Mr. Arty. I . . . have homework."

The thieves are fast, but they're no match for Spider-Man! He quickly catches the criminals, but by the time he hands them over to the police, Mr. Arty is long gone.

Miles can't help but wonder: How can he learn more about art if he's so busy being Spider-Man?

After he disappeared in the middle of their last conversation, Miles has trouble getting Mr. Arty to open up to him again. He tells his parents about Mr. Arty and asks for advice. "I want to learn more about art from a real artist, but he won't talk to me anymore."

His mami says, "Maybe find something else he enjoys that he's more open to talking about."

"Like what?" Miles asks.

"I know you'll think of something clever," she says.

Over the next few haircut Thursdays, Miles tries to get Mr. Arty to talk to him. Finally, he figures out how to put that spark in Mr. Arty's eyes again.

"Mr. Arty, do you know how to dance bomba?" Miles asks.

"Do I know bomba?" Mr. Arty says sarcastically. "You should see my moves at the class I go to in Williamsburg."

Miles challenges Mr. Arty.
"Oh yeah? I bet your moves
aren't as good as mine."

"Come see for yourself.
I go on Tuesday evenings,"
Mr. Arty says.

The next Tuesday, with Mami by his side, Miles and Mr. Arty dance the rhythm of the drums with master bomberos. Mr. Arty smiles the entire time.

After bomba class, Mr. Arty takes them to his favorite restaurant. Soon, Miles is hunched over a huge plate of mofongo with pork, the national Puerto Rican dish and a favorite from Arty's childhood—and Miles's own. It's sweet, savory, and warm, and tastes like home.

"You're right, this is the best mofongo ever," Miles says between bites.

"Watch it, kiddo," Mami jokes.

Later that night, when Miles is patrolling as Spider-Man, he swings through the city with the beat of the maracas from the dance class echoing in his ears.

Miles and Mr. Arty become good friends and go on lots of adventures around Brooklyn. "Art is life, and there is life all around Brooklyn," Mr. Arty says. "It's important we celebrate all the colors and the spaces it brightens while we can."

"What if you don't know how?" Miles asks. "What if you're not sure where your place is?"

"Everyone has something to give," Mr. Arty says. "You just have to figure out what that looks like for you. In fact, I want to show you something."

Mr. Arty brings Miles to a mural.

"This is my favorite mural," Miles begins. "It reminds me of all the things Mami says about her life as a kid back in Puerto Rico. I'm puertorriqueño and an artist. It is my calling, and I carry it in my heart."

Mr. Arty has tears in his eyes. "This is what I wanted to show you." He points at the artist's signature.

ARTY G.

Miles realizes his calling is to use his powers to make the world a better place.

"Thank you for being my friend," Miles says warmly.

"No, Miles. Thank you for being mine," says Mr. Arty.

Mr. Arty hands Miles a paintbrush. "Show me what you can do," he says.

Miles hesitates. He's never shared his art with anyone before. But Mr. Arty has taught him that being who he is, even if he's still figuring that out, means honoring his talents. All of them.

Mr. Arty smiles. "I'm going to call this one *Through Miles's Eyes*. Let's paint what moves us."

Later that week, Spider-Man comes across Mr. Arty again, showing their art to his friends. He wouldn't be Mr. Arty without being an artist, and Miles wouldn't be Miles without being Spider-Man.

Like Puerto Rico, like Brooklyn, Miles must hold Spider-Man in his heart, ALWAYS.